# THE
# GIFT OF
# *ALOHA*

Written and illustrated by Gill McBarnet

For Tara

First published 1996 by Ruwanga Trading
Distributed by Booklines Hawaii Ltd.

ISBN 0-9615102-9-3
©1996 Gill McBarnet

*L*ong ago, in the days when menehune roamed the cool green forests of Hawaii and fairies lived in the fragrant flowers, there once lived a king and queen who were loved by their people. They had ruled wisely and well for many years, but the time had come for their young son to become king.

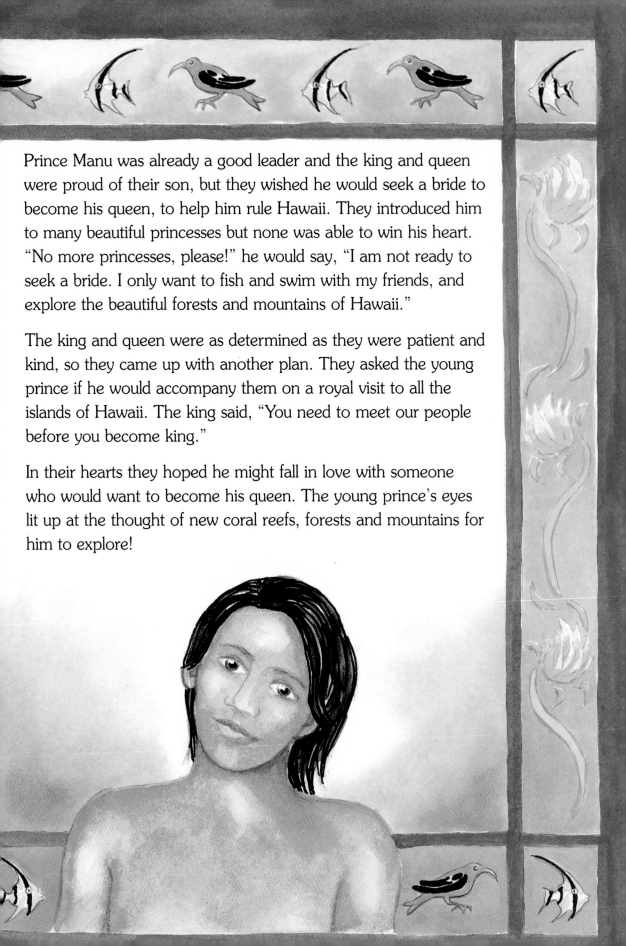

Prince Manu was already a good leader and the king and queen were proud of their son, but they wished he would seek a bride to become his queen, to help him rule Hawaii. They introduced him to many beautiful princesses but none was able to win his heart. "No more princesses, please!" he would say, "I am not ready to seek a bride. I only want to fish and swim with my friends, and explore the beautiful forests and mountains of Hawaii."

The king and queen were as determined as they were patient and kind, so they came up with another plan. They asked the young prince if he would accompany them on a royal visit to all the islands of Hawaii. The king said, "You need to meet our people before you become king."

In their hearts they hoped he might fall in love with someone who would want to become his queen. The young prince's eyes lit up at the thought of new coral reefs, forests and mountains for him to explore!

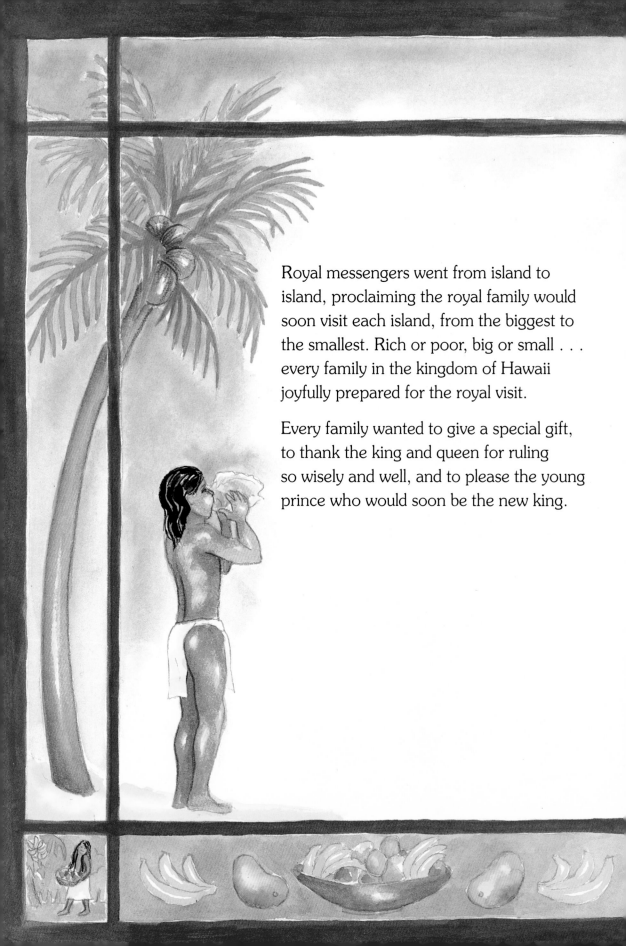

Royal messengers went from island to island, proclaiming the royal family would soon visit each island, from the biggest to the smallest. Rich or poor, big or small . . . every family in the kingdom of Hawaii joyfully prepared for the royal visit.

Every family wanted to give a special gift, to thank the king and queen for ruling so wisely and well, and to please the young prince who would soon be the new king.

On one of the smallest islands there lived a poor young girl named Leilani who had been raised by her grandmother. Her grandmother had become old and frail, so Leilani took care of her. She worked hard, gathering whatever food she could, from forest and seashore. Leilani knew the island like the back of her slender hand and although times were hard, she carried herself with grace and dignity.

Her smile expressed the happiness she had in her heart. She was happy and confident . . . until everyone started preparing for the royal visit.

As Leilani watched other families prepare their gifts, her heart grew sad because she wished she had something special to give. Everyone else had such wonderful gifts, but she felt she had nothing worthy to give. Wistfully, Leilani watched the activity in the village.

Kimo the fisherman and his family went out in their canoes, and returned with baskets brimming with fish. From the deep blue sea beyond the reefs, they fished for the big and sleek ulua, ahi . . . and the golden mahimahi. All fit for the royal platter!

The Pahulu family used their nets and spears in the coral reefs, to fish for the colorful manini, kumu and humuhumu-nukunuku-a-pua'a.

The delicious, colorful fish were sure to please the royal family.

Over many years, the Kekona family had gathered feathers from the birds of the forest. Like gleaming jewels, the feathers were carefully unpacked and placed in soft piles according to color . . . mainly orange and red.

"I knew a time would come when we could use our fine feathers . . ." Tutu Kekona said, as she and her family skillfully made a splendid helmet and cape for the king.

Hoku the taro farmer and his family
harvested their best taro plants, and
pounded the roots into the finest poi,
making it just the right thickness for
the royal family. "We will offer the poi,
along with our nicest poi pounder,"
the proud farmer announced.

Malia's family grew the finest fruit on
the island, and they picked only their
best bananas, mangoes, pineapples
and breadfruit. The tasty fruit was sure
to delight the royal family.

The Nihoa family used their skills and materials to print bold designs on beautifully worked pieces of tapa for the queen.

They also took long strips of dried lauhala, and with expert fingers they wove the lauhala into golden mats which would look beautiful in the royal home.

Kainoa and his family used a stately
koa tree to make a royal canoe . . .

. . . while the Kahana family made a
new surfboard for the prince. Long
and streamlined, they could picture
him catching wave after wave on the
sleek new board!

The Punahoa family used their musical skills to create musical instruments for the royal family. An ipu, drum and flute with which to play beautiful music.

They even had a magnificent conch to give to the young prince.

The families eagerly got their gifts ready for the royal visit. Leilani watched them working and listened to their talk and laughter. With a laugh, a group of young girls asked her "What gift do YOU have, Leilani?"

Sadly, Leilani walked into the forest. "I have nothing . . . no canoe or surfboard, tapa or lohala mat, drum or flute, feathered cape or helmet . . . I have none of these things! If only I had something beautiful to give the royal family when they come to our island . . ."

As she sat wishing and dreaming, she was suddenly surrounded by fairies. In a voice filled with the sweetness of birdsong, a fairy said. "With your generous heart and clever hands you have plenty to give! Look at the beautiful flowers around you. Why not make something with flowers?"

"Of course!" Leilani said excitedly. Seeing flowers hanging from a nearby branch she said "I could make a lei . . . using flowers . . . for each of our royal visitors!"

"We will help you." Said the fairies. More fairies appeared, and one by one they introduced themselves to Leilani and helped her to string the flowers of the forest into many beautiful leis.

Leilani no longer felt sad. She worked hard with her fairy friends, her nimble fingers threading the flowers with care and pride.

The plumeria fairies helped her pick plumeria blossoms with creamy white petals. Posies of pink plumeria glowed with the pink blush of a dawn sky above the mountains . . .

. . . and soon long lines of lilac and purple orchids were also threaded into colorful leis. The orchid fairies were a wonderful help, in their frilly hula skirts!

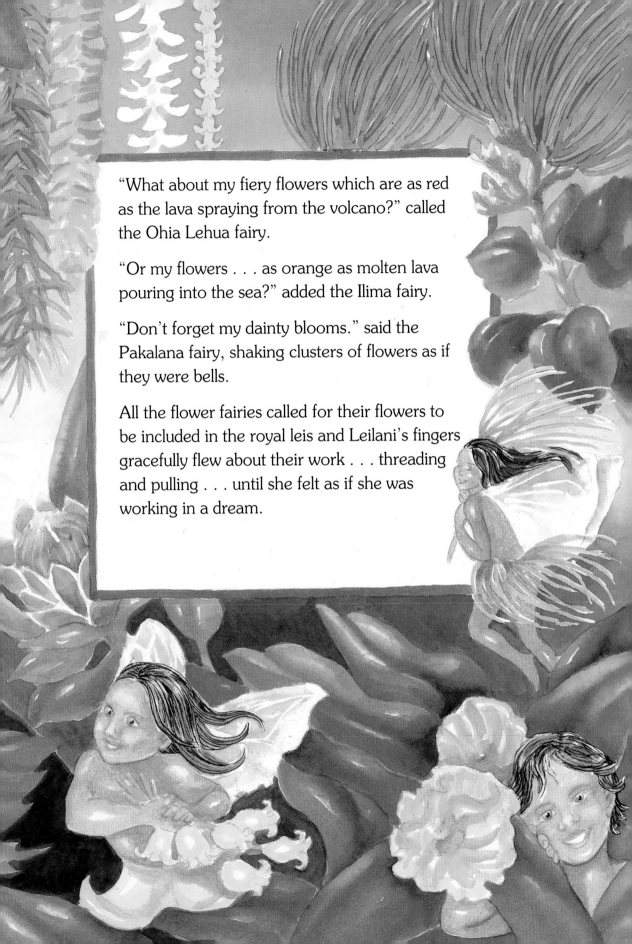

"What about my fiery flowers which are as red as the lava spraying from the volcano?" called the Ohia Lehua fairy.

"Or my flowers . . . as orange as molten lava pouring into the sea?" added the Ilima fairy.

"Don't forget my dainty blooms." said the Pakalana fairy, shaking clusters of flowers as if they were bells.

All the flower fairies called for their flowers to be included in the royal leis and Leilani's fingers gracefully flew about their work . . . threading and pulling . . . until she felt as if she was working in a dream.

The moon appeared in the evening sky.
A sprinkling of stars twinkled above like diamonds,
and still Leilani and her fairy friends worked on and
on. Threading and pulling, threading and pulling.

The air was sweet with the fragrance of tuberose,
ginger and pikake, when Leilani threaded the last
of the white petalled flowers. Like rows of silky
white stars they seemed to glow in the dim light as
Leilani thanked her fairy friends for all their help.
In a twinkle of stardust, each fairy disappeared as
quickly as he or she had appeared.

Happy and contented, Leilani fell asleep at last.

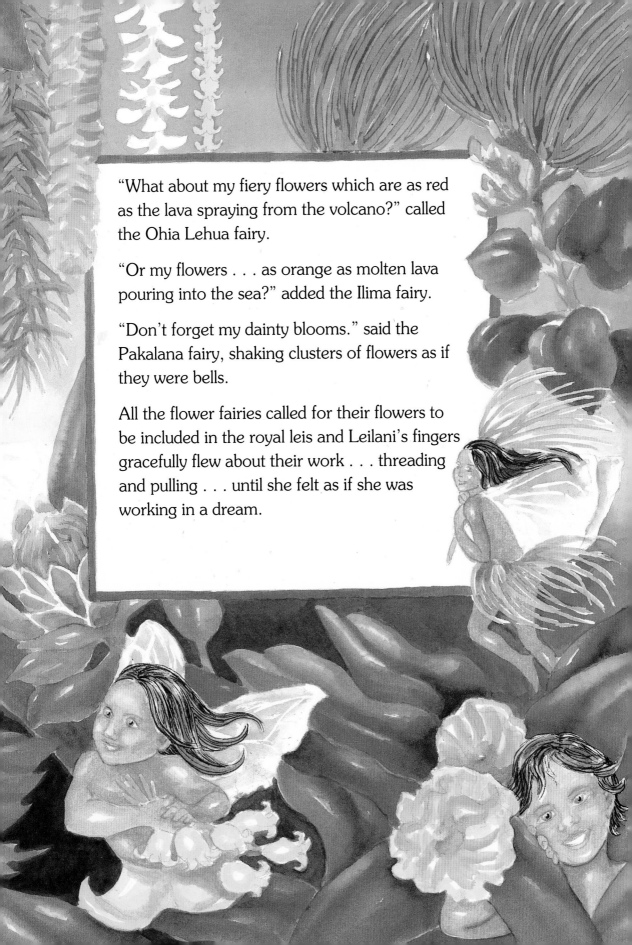

"What about my fiery flowers which are as red as the lava spraying from the volcano?" called the Ohia Lehua fairy.

"Or my flowers . . . as orange as molten lava pouring into the sea?" added the Ilima fairy.

"Don't forget my dainty blooms." said the Pakalana fairy, shaking clusters of flowers as if they were bells.

All the flower fairies called for their flowers to be included in the royal leis and Leilani's fingers gracefully flew about their work . . . threading and pulling . . . until she felt as if she was working in a dream.

The moon appeared in the evening sky.
A sprinkling of stars twinkled above like diamonds,
and still Leilani and her fairy friends worked on and
on. Threading and pulling, threading and pulling.

The air was sweet with the fragrance of tuberose,
ginger and pikake, when Leilani threaded the last
of the white petalled flowers. Like rows of silky
white stars they seemed to glow in the dim light as
Leilani thanked her fairy friends for all their help.
In a twinkle of stardust, each fairy disappeared as
quickly as he or she had appeared.

Happy and contented, Leilani fell asleep at last.

The next day dawned with the haunting cry of the conch, calling everyone down to the beach to greet the royal family. Gifts were given, and now it was Leilani's turn.

Gracefully she offered the royal family the fragrant and beautiful flower leis. "Aloha," she said in a voice that was warm and welcoming. Her smile was as friendly and bright as the morning sun, and the flower leis on her outstretched arms were as colorful as a rainbow. Nobody had ever made a lei from flowers before!

A hush fell on all who had gathered on the beach, because at that moment Leilani and her flowers looked absolutely lovely.

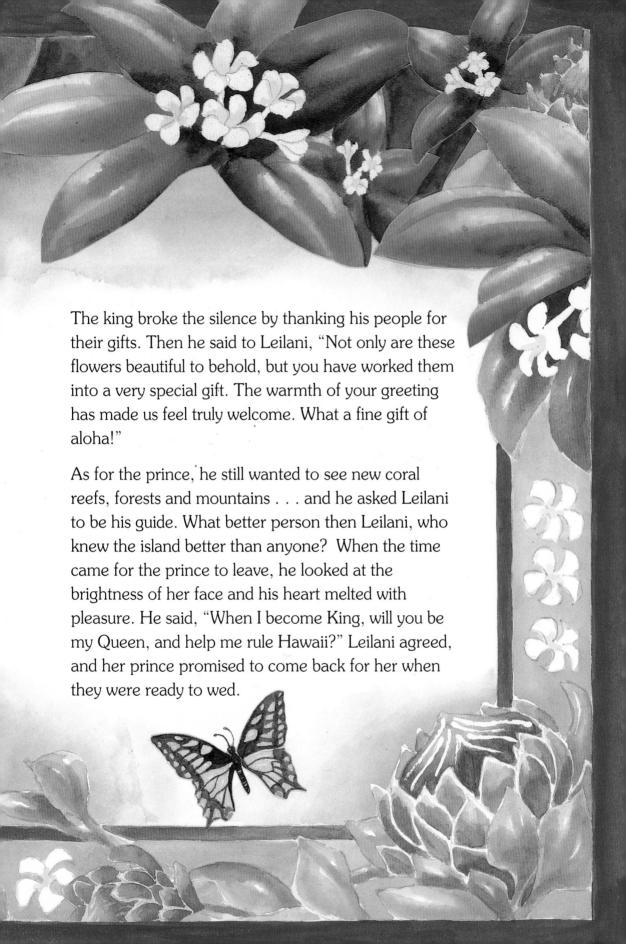

The king broke the silence by thanking his people for their gifts. Then he said to Leilani, "Not only are these flowers beautiful to behold, but you have worked them into a very special gift. The warmth of your greeting has made us feel truly welcome. What a fine gift of aloha!"

As for the prince, he still wanted to see new coral reefs, forests and mountains . . . and he asked Leilani to be his guide. What better person then Leilani, who knew the island better than anyone? When the time came for the prince to leave, he looked at the brightness of her face and his heart melted with pleasure. He said, "When I become King, will you be my Queen, and help me rule Hawaii?" Leilani agreed, and her prince promised to come back for her when they were ready to wed.

And he did. Some time later, when tuberose and plumeria flowers are at their most fragrant, the young king came back for his beautiful bride. Leilani became his queen and they lived happily ever after.

To this day, a flower lei is still the loveliest gift of aloha.

Also published by Ruwanga Trading:

*The Whale Who Wanted to be Small*
*The Wonderful Journey*
*A Whale's Tale*
*The Pink Parrot*
*Fountain of Fire*
*The Shark Who Learned a Lesson*
*The Goodnight Gecko*
*The Brave Little Turtle*
*Gecko Hide and Seek*


BOOK ORDERS AND ENQUIRIES:
Booklines Hawaii Ltd
94-527 Puahi Street
Waipahu, HI 96797